You must kiss a whale.

930265

■ one

I remember when it would rain during the summer, and the rain would stay on the pavement like a spill on the floor, and we could go outside in our bare feet, not putting on any extra clothes at all, no socks, no shoes, no hats or coats—when our neighborhood was just the largest room in our house. On rainy days like that, after the sun had set, my father would lead me to the street. At the edge of the asphalt we would crouch to see the puddled rain, the streetlights reflected within, and my father would say, It's like porcelain, see? The rain on the asphalt, filled with light. A thin shine you can break.

And then we would walk across the cool porcelain.

I am thirteen years old now. My name is Evelyn. Until a year ago I lived with my father, my mother, and my brother in a house in a suburb, a normal place with asphalt and streetlights and a corner where the school bus stopped every school day to pick us up. I had a friend then whose name was Michelle. I haven't heard from her since we moved a year ago, because out here there are no phones and the mailman never comes.

You see, we live in the desert, among the juniper trees and tumbleweeds, near the canyons, bluffs, and mesas. My mother brought us here soon after my father vanished (after he *died*, my mother says). She wanted to be near the storm. Yes, *the* storm. Maybe you've heard of it, maybe you haven't: the storm that circles through this desert once every month, as it has forever, always the same, always along the same path. The storm that is as permanent as the sun and the moon, and just as predictable. It's not a normal storm, after all. It's like an unhealing sore in the sky. And my mother wants to be near it. She especially wants to be near it, I think, *because* it is predictable. Predictable, that is, unlike my shiftless, absent father.

Our house is filled with clocks and calendars, so that we are prepared for every phase of the storm's coming, fury, and departure. Our almanac gives a thorough description of the storm. My mother has memorized this part of the almanac about the storm. With only a glance at a calendar and a clock she can tell me, and often does, how intense the storm is at that moment, and where, and how far away. Sometimes, in fact, before going out to her tent in our backyard (to continue her secret work), she will leave me some note that I will find at lunchtime, and that note will say, "The hail starts at 1:17 P.M.," or "Go out at 10:56 A.M. to see the lightning on the horizon," or something like that.

I mentioned Mother's secret work.

Mother had originally come out here intending to define and map out the storm, much as had the makers of the almanac, but to do it better, as if she were some weather Einstein. Again, she was counting on the *predictability* of the storm. She once told me a lie about her original intentions. She said that some time ago, before my brother had been born, she had tried to become a weather forecaster. She didn't want a job at a television station, she just wanted to predict the weather. So she bought a thermometer, a barometer, a wind sock, and other such things; she read a book, learning the names of all the clouds—cirrus, stratus, cumulonimbus; she reprogrammed her computer; and she set to work.

Unfortunately our city's weather was capricious. In fact, my mother said, it was downright *sentient*. It could *think*. And it was malicious, besides. It knew my mother was watching and set out to confuse her. In the backyard it would snow, in the front it would rain, and the sun would brighten the porch. There was thunder without lightning, and tornados in the distance without clouds in the sky.

My mother secretly monitored the pressure, the temperature, everything meteorological, but the air in her study betrayed her. It told the weather that a woman was coming to know too much, and the weather spitefully changed itself.

Our neighbors told my mother she was being a fool. Why, years ago the local television news had itself surrendered and replaced the weather report with an astrology report.

My mother surrendered only after the weather put a cloud over her head and kept her drenched every hour of the day. Her socks became squishy, her dinner was washed from her plate, and her bed became a pool. My father, wet as she, complained and told her to give up, and so reluctantly she did.

The moral of my mother's lie was, Never trust sentient weather.

■ ■

Now, the storm cannot think at all. It never even changes, mindlessly, like normal weather. After my father vanished, my mother became obsessed with the storm, for *there* was something that would not be capricious, would not change to spite her, would not ever make her surrender. The storm she could predict with absolute certainty.

But she soon discovered she could not define the storm or map it any better than had the makers of the almanac. Although her predictions were good, there was really no point to her work, and she became very discouraged.

Until, that is, she decided to *fight* the storm. And how do you fight a storm? By not allowing it to ruin your day. By not allowing it to keep you trapped inside the house. My mother has set out to make a raincoat that even the great and violent perpetual storm cannot defeat.

And that is her secret work: She is out in her tent, making the Ultimate Raincoat. It's a secret because she won't tell me. She says if I know, it will jinx the project. She's tried eight times already, and each of those eight times I knew what sort of raincoat she was making and how it was progressing, and each of those eight times the storm ignored her newest raincoat and knocked her down and nearly drowned her. So Mother concluded that I was a jinx, and now tells me nothing at all.

■ ■

I rarely see my mother. I see her only when we awaken, have breakfast, have dinner, and go to bed. All the rest of the time she is in her tent.

So I have to take care of my baby brother Zack, who is just over a year old. I don't mind caring for him, since he's pretty quiet. Of course he doesn't talk. Sometimes we exchange noises, *dee dee, booba doo,* that sort of nonsense, but we never talk. Well, I do talk *to* him, but he never answers because he can't, and I don't expect an answer anyway.

I tend to keep him with me all day long. I have a papoose, which is comfortable on me, and in which he sleeps very well. There's really not much to do in this house but carry Zack around, although while carrying him I do try to wander through the broken rooms, where, at least, it isn't completely boring.

Our house, you see, has broken rooms. The storm has broken them. Our house has rooms like an onion has rings, and every month the outer rooms, the ones on the fringe, are chewed up and spat out by the storm. The house itself survives because it's huge. The inner rooms get shaken and wet, but survive. And the mob of tornados brought by the storm never touches our house, which was built, by whoever built it, to be within the storm, but never to be destroyed by it.

I don't know who built our house, or why they did. The house is abandoned, has been so for years, and we are only squatters.

■■

So I walk with Zack through the broken rooms. I know this is probably dangerous, but I do it anyway. No one is here to stop me. I walk carefully, in any event, and avoid any roof that seems to be buckling. I walk around the sprinkled glass. And I stay on the first floor, by and large, at least when Zack is with me (I sometimes do go alone), so that I don't step onto some weakened board and fall through to the rest of the debris.

I think a lot in the broken rooms, I think a lot about a lot of things. I think about Michelle. And when I say to Zack, "Look at the pattern those fallen beams have made," of course he just makes some noise and squirms sleepily in his papoose.

One day I found a broken room that, unlike the others, had more in it than parts of itself. There was a chest, and in that chest were all sorts of things, a few of which I recognized from long ago. The chest can only be my mother's. It was not locked, it was not hidden behind or under anything, but for some reason my mother has put it far from the inner rooms where we sleep and eat. I doubt that she has touched it since.

There was a small stack of papers in the chest, old papers covered with my father's handwriting. My father's handwriting is terrible, it is very dense on the paper and strung out in wavy lines, like sediment. Many lines and parts of lines have been crossed out, some with replacements scrawled in the margins.

At first I couldn't figure out what my father had been writing down on all those pieces of paper. It has taken me a while, but I have discovered that at least the first few pages are a *story*. The story begins like this:

> Kevin got a letter one day that said, You must kiss a whale. The letter didn't start with Dear Kevin, it didn't end with Sincerely Yours, it didn't have any sentences on it besides the one, and that one said, You must kiss a whale.
>
> The paper was folded only once, crookedly,

and seemed to have been wet, but was dry and crinkled now. The writing on the paper and on the envelope was careless, messy, barely legible. The postmark told Kevin that the letter had come, or at least had been mailed, from a nearby coastal town.

Kevin couldn't imagine who would have sent him this letter.

Nor could he imagine why he should kiss a whale.

I confess that I've had to be creative with what my father has written, since it is so . . . well, barely legible. But although much of it may sound like me, those words above are essentially my father's.

My father's words! I never knew he wrote stories. Mother never told me. *He* never told me. I do miss my father. I think of the rain on the asphalt, of the shining porcelain, and I miss my father. But I resent this silence. Why didn't he tell me about his words? Why hasn't my mother told me about her chest? I feel like I am under some conspiracy of silence, and I get very lonely sometimes. I wish Mother would come in from her stupid tent.

■ two

The clouds today are the sort I like best, short piles of white with flat bottoms of gray, row after row across the sunny blue sky. My mother would know their scientific name. These clouds have nothing to do with the storm, they are common normal ones, and so I like them all the more. I went out and sat in a lawn chair, on the lawn we don't have (only sand and rocks and weeds surround our house); and with Zack in my lap, I listened to Mother hammering away and watched the clouds pass overhead.

■ ■

In Mother's chest, apart from Father's story,

there were many things. There were several flashlights, large and small, one with its batteries still
inside, now swollen and corroded. Mother used to
play with flashlights from the time she had been little, putting circles of light all around darkened
rooms. On winter mornings she'd wake me up for
school by shining a light across my face and whis-
pering my name.

In the chest there was also a pencil case that
Mother had given to me in third grade. It has a pic-
ture on it of a smiling tomato, and above the tomato
it says, *I am not a watermelon.*

There was a string of seven tiny copper bells.

There was a scarecrow doll.

There was, in fact, so much that I haven't finished
going through it all. It would be easier, I guess, if I
could just dump the chest onto the floor, but I can't
do that because it seems to me that everything has
been put into the chest very neatly. Mother might
someday return to this chest and I don't want her to
notice my tampering, so I am very careful, taking
out one thing at a time and putting it back where it
was.

Fortunately Father's story was right on top, so I
can take it out and put it back without any problems. Every day I go to the chest and take out my

father's story, and from his horrible handwriting I've reconstructed this:

The day that Kevin got the letter, he was sick. He had been very sick for several days. A week before, he'd had only a little cold, which had seemed to be fading away. But then one night he went out, and it was dismally raining, and his cold, prompted by the dismal rain, stopped fading away and filled up his head and his chest.

So these days he was at home, sick.

The first couple of days he had stayed in bed, sleeping in bits and pieces. His mother wanted to take him to the doctor. Kevin refused to go. Since he didn't have a fever and was keeping down what little food he ate, his mother didn't bring up the doctor again.

His mother normally worked. She was an administrative assistant at some corporation. But with Kevin sick, she had gotten some time off. She didn't mind. In fact, she seemed to enjoy tending to Kevin. She would come to his bedroom door every quarter hour, and poke her head into the room, and see if Kevin was sleeping soundly, or restlessly, or if he was awake. And if he was awake, she would ask him what he needed, was he hungry, or thirsty, did he want a book to read. She would come in and fix up his covers so that they covered him better. She adjusted the window blinds, more open or more closed, depending on the sunlight coming in. And always she lay the back of her hand against his forehead to check for fever, and always she spoke softly so that Kevin was never jarred by her voice.

Someone else visited Kevin during the day, and that was his younger brother Matt. Matt was too young for school, and normally he went to their grandmother's house during the day, while Mother was at work. But since Mother was staying home these days, Matt was staying home, too. And although he was young, he was quite old enough to walk, talk, and be obnoxious.

When Mother wasn't looking, Matt would come into Kevin's bedroom and throw something at Kevin. Like a rubber ball. Or he would bring a toy sword and stab at Kevin. Or he would drive a toy tank over Kevin. He always sniveled and made faces. He called Kevin ugly boy, ugly boy, because of his red and tired face and runny nose. When Kevin would yell at Matt to get out, his yell choked on his cold and became a gurgling rasp. When he would throw the ball back, Matt laughed and evaded it. And all the while Kevin was trapped in his bed.

Mother would soon come and grab Matt by his shirt or his belt and lift him away from Kevin. She hissed at Matt to leave his poor brother alone. Matt would thrash and whine. Mother would lock Matt up in his own room, but that wouldn't last long, since Matt would scream and scream and keep Kevin from resting. So Mother had to let him out, but she told him to behave or else.

Finally Kevin was well enough to come out of his bedroom. Still, he didn't move much, sitting almost all day in front of the television, even when it was off. Sometimes he played video games, but not much. Matt, on the other hand, played as many video games as he could, even if their noises were worsening Kevin's headache. Matt would also come up behind the couch, sneering ugly, ugly, ugly boy, and jab Kevin in the head.

Mother brought Kevin magazines and drinks of water or pop. She brought him the letter from the coastal town. "Who do you know there?" she asked Kevin, and he just shrugged, he didn't know anyone there. Curious, his mother started to open the letter, but Kevin protested since it was his, and so she gave it to him, unopened.

That's all, for now. I stopped to take a rest. Of course there's a lot more to reconstruct.

Sometimes I do wonder if my father really wrote, I mean composed, *created*, this story. He must have, though. I don't recognize it, and I've read a lot, and been taught a lot. It's certainly his handwriting in any event. I've made certain of that. You see, I got out this letter he sent me when I was very young, and which I have kept, and in which he wrote this:

> My dearest daughter Evelyn,
> I haven't seen you in so long, and there you are, already two years old. How the war keeps me away! But I do think of you, out on patrol. When I worry about the enemy over the ridge and in the trees I think of you and I worry less. The picture of you that I carry keeps the enemy away from me. My darling Evelyn, the war can't last forever. Soon I will be home with you.

My father was not in any war. He was never even in the army. He had simply run away from us, as he would again. I was eight when I found this letter in a dresser drawer, among some photographs. I think my mother had overlooked it. Perhaps she once intended to give it to me and so set it aside, but then decided to leave it aside, and then forgot about it, along with those photographs of her and Father and me, newborn.

Anyway, I compared the letter and the story, and I assure you that they were written with the same hand, my father's—just as they were written with the same amount of make-believe.

■■

This morning, between breakfast and lunch, I took Zack with me in our pickup truck. He drove. That is, I sat him in the driver's seat and buckled him in. Of course he couldn't reach the steering wheel; and his feet, of course, couldn't reach the pedals; and we, of course, went nowhere at all. But sitting in the pickup was something to do.

The pickup is parked way inside the house, inside a former living room, to keep it protected from the storm. We've cleared a very long and twisting driveway down a hall and through some broken rooms. The driveway ends out on the lawn. When the storm is on the other side of the desert and it's peaceful here, Mother takes the pickup into Soso, the nearest town, to get supplies. Sometimes she takes me and Zack, if I notice that she's going and I ask her to take us.

While Zack and I were in the pickup today, I heard Mother somewhere inside the house, calling for us. This was unusual, since she rarely leaves her tent before dinner. I didn't know what to think. It was the wrong time of the day to be hearing her voice, and because I was confused, I didn't answer her.

She finally appeared in the driveway, right outside the living room. She saw me through the windshield. I could tell she was up to something, because she was agitated, moving like she does when she's agitated, like a worried mouse. She smiled, but then she made a funny face and looked rapidly left and right. She was looking for Zack, who was hidden behind the steering wheel. When Zack made a noise and Mother heard him, she realized he was in the pickup with me, and her funny face went away.

Mother came over to the pickup. She had a measuring tape in her hand. She said, "Evelyn, get Zack, come out here, I need to do something, hurry," and then she added, "please." I unbuckled Zack and we got out.

She told me to hold Zack under his arms and

stand him up. I did. Then she measured everything of his that she could: his height, his width, his depth; his arms, his legs, his fingers; his neck, his head, his nose; everything, all of him. When she was done with Zack she told me to sit him down on the floor and stand myself up, straight. I did. She then measured me as she had measured Zack. She didn't have to write down our dimensions. She memorized them as she took them. All the time she was measuring, she muttered things I couldn't understand.

When she was done with me she left. I watched her leaving. I didn't say a word, since Mother was still muttering to herself, and I figured any questions would only bother her. But then I decided I *wanted* to know, and so, before Mother was out of sight, I asked, "Why did you measure us?"

She stopped and turned. She looked at me for a very long time. Normally, since I'm a jinx, she'd have simply ignored me. But then again, she had never so directly involved me (or Zack) in her raincoat-making before. Maybe this once she actually *owed* me an explanation.

Finally my mother said, "I have to get my raincoat the right size. You and Zack are the *wrong* size. I have to know how big *not* to make my raincoat."

That was it, the all of it, odd logic and all. My mother was gone, gone back to her tent, and I now had the absurd answer to my question.

I spent the next ten minutes trying to get Zack out from under the pickup. He had crawled under there as Mother and I had exchanged sentences.

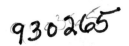

It looks like I'll miss the eighth grade again. I missed it last year. Legally I should have been in school, of course, but legally we shouldn't be in this house, either. I believe Mother has not even considered the legality of all she's done. She's certainly not a *criminal*, but my truancy and our trespassing seem to have slipped her notice. In any event, though summer's ending I don't think I'll have to worry about textbooks or homework any time soon.

Without school I have been bored at times. Not that I was ever keen on school, but it *was* something to do. This past year I've done little but take care of Zack.

At least now I'm busy. I just reconstructed another chunk of Father's story. I hope I finish it all before the storm gets here. I won't be able to sneak off to Mother's chest once she is back in the house, with me and Zack in the inner rooms.

Anyhow, here's the latest chunk:

Once, Mother thought she felt a fever on Kevin and dabbed his face with a cool, damp cloth. This annoyed Kevin, since all it really did was make his face wet. His mother, however, was not hurt when he complained about the cloth. She went on in her business, comforting her sick little boy.

Matt began mimicking Kevin's sickness. He sniffled loudly. He faked coughs and sneezes. He slumped on the couch, like Kevin, and pouted, boo hoo hoo, ugly, ugly. Kevin told him to go away. Matt didn't go. Kevin swung his fist at him, but Matt just ducked and still didn't go. So Kevin tried to ignore him. He watched television. He managed to nap. And he studied the letter that said, You must kiss a whale.

The writing, as I have said, was messy. Kevin wanted to be certain of every word, so he followed the scratchings of ink very carefully. Y O U You. M U S T Must. K I S . . . Kevin hesitated here. That S was quite messy. It almost didn't look like an S. It didn't really look like the S in *must*. But it must have been an S. So . . . S S . . . The next S was as bad as the one before. But still . . . K I S S Kiss. A. That was definitely an A. *You must kiss a.* And the last word could be nothing except *whale.* In fact, it was the only word that even approached neatness.

No matter how many times Kevin studied the letter, every time he came up with nonsense. Only that third word, which he assumed was *kiss,* ever wavered. Sometimes, when he read it, it was clearly *kiss.* Other times it was something else.

Once it seemed to him that it was *kill.*

At least he was getting healthier, day by day. Mother was pleased. Matt was not. Matt became more irksome. The rubber ball again. The toy tanks. The sword.

Kevin became infuriated enough to yell an Extremely Foul Word at Matt, a word that even adults were not supposed to say. The Word astonished Matt. He knew what it was, and how bad it was. It stopped him dead. For a moment he just stared at Kevin, who stared angrily back. And then Matt, figuring that Kevin was in big trouble now, ran to Mother to tattle.

Kevin fumed where he sat. He expected to get an unpleasant talking-to. That would be an unwelcome change from his mother's recent comfort and cheer.

But it didn't happen that way.

Mother came reluctantly with Matt. She

assumed he was just making trouble as usual. She told him she was busy; she told him to leave Kevin alone. But Matt just kept pulling her toward the couch.

"He said it, Mom, he said it!"

"Said what?" she wearily asked Matt, when they stood in front of Kevin.

And Matt said the Word.

"Matt!" Mother yelped.

"But Mom, he said it, he said it!"

"Look, young man," she said, wagging a finger at Matt, "you have been a first-class pest for a week. Now cut it out."

"But Mom! Kevin said—" and Matt said the Word again.

"Matt!" she snapped. "Don't say that!"

"But Mom—"

"And leave your brother alone!"

"But Mom—"

"That does it, young man. You're going to your room and staying there forever. No matter how much you scream."

Matt whimpered as Mother dragged him away.

Kevin watched them leave, and grinned.

It was amazing what a difference one word could make.

Kevin was recovered, at least enough to return to school. But although his mother thought he was going to school this morning, in fact he was not. He was going to the coastal town.

The letter had occupied him more and more as his sickness had faded. Its nonsense angered Kevin. And he resented whoever had sent it. He resented them for being anonymous and for disrupting his days with mysterious absurdity. He was going to find them and demand that they explain themselves.

He especially resented the messiness of the letter. He had to know if it was saying *kiss,* or if it was saying *kill.*

So while his mother made his lunch (hastily, of course, since she had to get to work), Kevin sneaked into his parents' bedroom and used their phone to call for a cab. He told the cab to meet him at a certain corner that was three blocks from his home. Then he went into his brother's bedroom—Matt was already gone because Dad, on his way to work, had dropped him off at Grandma's house—and from his brother's bank Kevin stole every single coin. Matt's money, along with Kevin's own, would surely be enough to pay the fare for the cab.

Kevin kissed his mother, left the house, and

walked to the corner to meet the cab. His mother drove past him on her way to work. She beeped the horn and waved, and Kevin, innocently acting like any boy on his way to school, backpack on his back, lunch bag in his hand, waved back to his mom, and nodded, and smiled. Then his mother turned into a side-street and was gone.

Kevin had to wait at the corner for only a few minutes. At first, when the cabbie did arrive, he ignored Kevin, circling around the block twice because he had expected to pick up an adult. The cabbie finally stopped and asked Kevin, "Hey, kid, you seen any grown-ups around here?" Kevin told him, "I'm the one who wants the ride." The cabbie smirked and said, "Oh? Missed your bus?" Kevin petulantly said no, he hadn't missed his bus; he wasn't going to school at all. And then he showed the cabbie his money. The cabbie hesitated. He asked Kevin, "Well, where are you going?" Kevin told him: The coastal town. The cabbie said, "That's kind of far away, isn't it?" Kevin answered him with an impatient tilt of his head. The cabbie hesitated again. He looked left and right to make sure there really weren't any adults waiting for him. Then he shrugged and said, "Okay, kid, get in," and Kevin did.

They were out of the neighborhood and on a major street when the cabbie asked, "Do your parents know where you're going?"

Kevin lied, "Of course."

"Why aren't they with you?"

"They're at work."

"Oh."

A few minutes later, the cabbie asked, "Where exactly in the town do you want to go?"

"The coast part, I guess."

"The coast part?"

"Yeah. On the ocean. The coast."

"Oh."

A few minutes after that, the cabbie said, "It's kind of a long trip, you know."

"I know."

"Do you mind if I talk?"

"What?"

"Talk. Do you mind if I talk?"

"I guess." Kevin looked out the window.

"Great. I like talking."

"Whatever."

"What?"

"Whatever you like. Talk if you want."

The cabbie smirked. "How old are you, anyway?"

"Asking me questions is not talking."

"Well, do you mind conversing, then?"

"Yes."

"Oh. Well, at least tell me your name."

Kevin stared at the cabbie. Then he lied: "Brian."

"Well, Brian, if you won't converse, I'll talk."

"Like I said, talk if you want."

And so the cabbie did talk, about this and that; and not once did he tire of talking to himself.

"Want some gum?" the cabbie asked.

Kevin didn't, so he said no.

They were almost to the town. The trip had, indeed, been a long one, and for most of it Kevin had kept to himself. The cabbie, for his part, had talked his way down to short-winded phrases, nothing more sophisticated than "Want some gum?" or "Nice day out, isn't it?" or "Hey, we're almost there."

The cabbie seemed much too cheerful to Kevin. Kevin didn't trust the cabbie's sort of friendliness. It was more strange to him than welcome. But of course he had to put up with it, since he was in the cabbie's cab.

The letter, meanwhile, continued to anger Kevin.

It confused him. He fumed over it. A small part of Kevin, a part all fiery and spiteful, tried very hard to convince Kevin that the letter said, quite obviously, *kill*. Kill a whale. With everything possible, said the small part of Kevin. Knives. Hand grenades. Submachine guns. Intercontinental ballistic missiles. Blam, splatter, dead—said the cruel part of Kevin.

Then it occurred to Kevin that the letter and the cabbie were equally strange. Neither one was quite right somehow. It occurred to Kevin that perhaps he should take advantage of this fact. Besides, the cabbie clearly liked Kevin. And he was a lot older than Kevin. Maybe he could help.

"Um, mister . . . "

"Yes, Brian?"

Kevin bit his lip. "Um. My name's Kevin."

"Oh?" said the cabbie, smiling.

"Um. Yeah."

"Okay then, Kevin. What's up?"

"Can you help me with something?"

"What's that?"

"Well . . . " *How to explain this?* "Well, I got this letter."

"Yes?"

"The letter's why I'm going to the coastal town."

"Oh?"

"Yeah. And it says I have to kiss a whale."

"The letter?"

"Yes."

"It says you have to kiss a whale?"

"Yeah. Either that, or kill one."

"Kill one? Can't you tell?"

"No. Whoever wrote it doesn't write very neatly."

"Let me see it."

Kevin handed the letter to the cabbie. The cabbie, eyes still on the road, reached over, fumbled a bit, then glanced at Kevin's outstretched hand and grabbed the letter. For a minute or so he alternated between reading the letter and watching the traffic. Then he handed the letter back to Kevin.

"You're right. It's not very neat."

"What do you think it says?"

"It's very strange."

"I know. But what do you think?"

"I can't tell either. It's sloppy."

Kevin sighed. "Well, who would have sent it?"

The cabbie shrugged. "I have no idea."

Kevin frowned. So much for the cabbie's help.

"You know," said the cabbie, "there's a university in town."

"So?"

"Well, they have a pretty good language department. I bet if you took that letter to them, they could tell you what it says. Analyze it, you know. Maybe what you think is *whale* isn't. Maybe *whale* is actually a foreign word that only looks English."

Kevin, frowning, thought about that.

"In any event," said the cabbie, "before we go to the coast I can take you to Morrill Hall."

"What hall?"

"Morrill Hall. At the university. It's where the language department is."

"How do you know?"

"I went to that university."

"Oh."

So the cabbie had been to college.

That explained his strangeness.

I had to stop there. Father's handwriting got horrendously messy, and I was in no mood to fight it. But I've got only two weeks to get it right. Although, right now, the sky is blue and empty, I know this is only the calm before.

I was in a broken room today and I found one of Mother's earlier Ultimate Raincoats. It's shaped like a cone, six feet high, and covered with heavy chains. The chains are for weight, to keep you from being blown away. The cone is made of thick plastic that rainwater runs right off of. Since the coat is so heavy it has these little grabber feet, mechanical claws that pull you along the ground when you push a button, and grip the ground when you don't. There are lenses in the cone so that you can see out, and mechanical arms so that you can pick things up or open doors.

When Mother wore this coat, about three months ago at the height of the storm, its electrical system shorted out, nearly electrocuting her. The wind pushed against the cone just enough to tip it and leave a gap between it and the ground—and then the wind got into the cone, blew Mother around inside, making her stumble, and the weight of the chains brought everything down.

I guess my mother has banished this coat, so broken itself, to a broken room. It *was* a terrible design. Sometimes Mother's desperation wrecks her ingenuity. She is normally quite good with things.

I don't know if Father's story is good or bad. I'm too busy rescuing it from his handwriting to make any kind of judgment. But it wouldn't matter anyhow if the story was ultimately junk. I'd reconstruct *any* story written by my father.

How many fathers, after all, write stories?

I suppose, in my father's case, it's not so astonishing. I mean, it's not so astonishing once you've accepted the fact that he did it. It's not like he was illiterate or hated books. He had so many books, and loved them all. The only job, in fact, that he had ever had was as a bookstore clerk. For the three years up until Zack's birth, Father never left us once, and he worked at a bookstore forty hours a week helping support his family. Mother, of course, had always worked. She designed computer software. We'd never suffered financially by Father's disappearances. It was certainly not the extra income Father brought in that delighted my mother; it was his dedication to a stable life. She was happy those three years.

And my father, I think, was happy as well.

I wonder if he wrote the story during those three years. I don't recall him writing then, or at any time for that matter, but perhaps he did it at night when the rest of us were asleep and not paying any attention.

It's actually hard to tell how old the papers are. For all I know, they could be older than me. Fourteen. My parents were married fourteen years ago. Maybe the papers are older than even that. Maybe they are left over from when my father was young.

Whatever their age, I'm still slogging through them. And I've got only a week and a half now. Today the first clouds, the wispy gray ones, the fringe of the storm, arrived.

■■

Today I made a huge mistake. I brought Zack with me to Mother's chest.

Normally I don't. Normally I go to the chest only in the afternoon, after I've put Zack down for his nap. I don't have to watch him then, and I can concentrate on Father's story. But today Zack was restless, he wouldn't sleep, he wouldn't let me leave. Oh, yes, I could have stayed with him and skipped a trip to Mother's chest—but then I'd have missed a day of work, and I don't have the time to lose anymore.

So I brought him along.

All was fine to begin with. Zack stayed happily enough on his blanket, there in the middle of the floor, ringed by the debris that I'd cleared away for him. He played with his toys. Meanwhile I sat next to a rip in the wall, under the sunlight muted gray, reconstructing Father's words. Occasionally I looked over to Zack, and each time he was where he had been, content on his blanket. I began to ignore him.

Then I heard a crash.

I looked up and saw Zack at the chest. He'd lifted himself up to stand at its rim and shoved his hand inside and scooped out lots of Mother's stuff. He was tugging the arms of the scarecrow doll. I screamed at him. Screeched, more like it. And he jumped. He started to cry.

I wasn't worried about Mother hearing him, no matter how much he cried. Out in her tent she heard nothing but herself. Still, Zack was crying an awful lot, and shaking because of it. But of course I'd screamed enough to terrify him. I was terrified myself. After all, he was destroying the neatness in Mother's chest.

I ran over to Zack and picked him up, to get him away from the chest, to try to calm him down. He kept on crying, sopping my shirt. I whispered to him, gentle tiny words, but he kept on crying like it was his last chance ever to cry. I finally gave up and put him down on his blanket, and sat cross-legged across from him, looking sad myself, trying to let him see I was sorry. That worked. He sniffled then, and nothing else.

He was, however, still holding the scarecrow doll.

Maybe I could have taken it from him, despite the grip he had on it. I could have traded one of his own toys for it. I could have, I even tried, but his crying surged back whenever I tried, and so I let him be.

I had no idea how everything had been arranged in the chest. I'd never memorized the layout. I had to put it all back mostly by guessing. The chest looked neat enough when I was done. I shut it tight, and although I couldn't lock it, and certainly wouldn't have anyhow (since I have no key), I did bury it under a fallen piece of the broken ceiling, a big piece that Zack couldn't remove.

Then I went back to Father's story.

Zack eventually fell asleep on his blanket, at long last took his nap. The rest of the afternoon he didn't disturb me once, and I did so much reconstructing that everything started to hurt: my eyes, my back, my writing hand. I was very tired when I decided to quit. I put back Father's story, put my own papers under my arm, and carefully picked up Zack, yawning dizzily while I did so. I absentmindedly collected all his toys into his blanket and left the broken room.

In short, I forgot about the scarecrow doll. It was there in the blanket with all of Zack's other toys. I didn't remember about it until dinner—and remembering about it gave me a sick jolt, since by that time, of course, Mother was right there at the dinner table, only one room away from a doll she had left, long ago, in a chest I was never meant to find.

■■

I had made dinner, as always. Spaghetti and salad. Sauce from a jar and torn lettuce in bowls. I make spaghetti and salad a lot, since it's easy, and I like it, and Mother couldn't care less what she eats, since food to her is just, as she puts it, fuel. I don't think she ever even *notices* what she's eating. Besides, spaghetti and salad are cheap, and although we have a fair amount of money (fifteen years of savings, removed from the bank a year ago), that money isn't limitless, and Mother tends to buy the simplest things she can, the same things, in fact, every time, and in the same amounts.

And the meals are simple as well, because the kitchen is simple—a stove that barely works, six or seven utensils, a couple of mixing bowls, some pots and pans—not a cook's kitchen at all, which is fine, since I'm not a cook. The kitchen had to be restored when we got there, and its restoration was never a priority with my mother. She got the electricity going (our house, out here in the desert, has its own generator), but fixing the stove never really has interested Mother. As mechanisms go, a stove is pretty uninteresting.

The utensils and such had been brought along on our move out here only as an afterthought. *Eating,* for Mother, has become an afterthought.

So anyhow, we were having dinner. Zack refused his strained peas. I shared my sauce with him. Mother ate slowly, her mind in other places. And then I remembered about the doll. The jolt had me spilling sauce on Zack, who, being a baby, didn't really mind the mess. Mother didn't see the sick look on my face, but it was there. The thought of the doll, one room away, screwed into my gut. I had to get that doll back to the chest. But I couldn't, not then, not until Mother had returned to her tent. I couldn't imagine why she should go into Zack's room before then. Surely she would never see the doll before I returned it. . .

But what if she . . .

And then Mother spoke. I heard her accuse, con-
vict, and sentence me; but she didn't. She didn't even
speak to me, as such. She was just musing aloud.

"Monsters," she said, and paused.

For a ridiculous moment during Mother's pause,
I feared that the doll would make some noise, give
itself away, cough or laugh or cry out for help. It
didn't.

Mother said, "The weather made *monsters*."

Zack would say something. I knew it. By accident. Not to get me in trouble, but just because,
how could he know? He'd innocently ask to play
again with the scarecrow doll. But Zack can't talk.
He just poked his fingers in the sauce that I had
spilled on him and on his high-chair tray.

"Monsters!" my mother lied. I knew what she
was talking about. She'd told me long ago that in
her hometown, during the hardest rains, the clouds
would sag and reach like icicles, and touch the
ground, and then thicken and curdle into monsters,
all mouth and claw and constant roar. They had no
eyes, and so were blind. They devoured whatever
they fell upon. They were huge, and their jaws
wrenched apart everything, their teeth tore open
everything, their tongues yanked everything out of
sight. The monsters fed on Mother's hometown,

while the people either ran away or hid and prayed.

I knew all this. Mother has told me that lie before. She's told me many others like it. I've certainly never believed any of them, but I don't think she even wants my belief. A lie's just another of her contraptions. Mother's always making things, out of metal, out of plastic, out of mislaid thoughts, and sometimes I just get to see what she has made; sometimes I get to hear her lies.

But today over dinner, Mother didn't go into detail. She only said, "Monsters. The weather made *monsters*. Monsters! So I guess I should be grateful that the storm brings only wind and hail and a hundred tornados, eh, Evelyn?"

I didn't know what to say. There wasn't much *to* say. Yet I was especially speechless because of her manner. Mother wasn't even looking at me. Her voice had been . . . odd. She was tapping her fingers on the table. Then she got up suddenly, her dinner unfinished, and went back outside to her work. She never even suspected my intrusion into her chest, nor the misadventure with her scarecrow doll. But how could she have? She was worrying about monsters, and she was much too tired and sad.

▬▬

I don't like it. Mother has no right to be sad. She's

a maniac. A maniac with a tent and two neglected children. But she was sad. It was obvious. And I don't like it. What am I supposed to make of a sad maniac? Maybe *I* can be sad, but she certainly can't. She's just a maniac, pure and simple. Mother has no right to be anything else.

At least she never went into Zack's room. As soon as she was gone I got the doll and shoved it under my bed, under some old magazines. Tomorrow I'll put it back. And if Zack doesn't want to take his nap, I'll just have to kill him. The little jerk.

■ three

Here is some more of Father's story:

The cabbie, waiting cheerfully outside Morrill Hall, was leaning against his cab and watching the students going to class. He had told Kevin to go in and see Professor Lopez. Kevin had asked the cabbie to accompany him, but the cabbie declined, saying he had never turned in his final research paper to Professor Lopez and was still embarrassed about it. Besides, he wanted to stay outside in the sun. It was autumn, "and there're few things lovelier," said the cabbie, "than a campus on a sunny autumn day."

Kevin wasn't exactly intimidated by seeing the professor on his own. He just didn't know what she would be like. Besides, his cold was acting up again. He was sniffling. He didn't want to sniffle in front of a professor.

In any event, he read the building directory and found out that Professor Lopez was in room 301. He took the stairs to the third floor. No one tried to stop him—apparently you didn't need a hall pass in college. Of course, some students did give him funny looks, since Kevin was only ten.

The third floor was quiet. A window at the end of the hall was open. The papers tacked to the bulletin boards lifted in the breeze. Kevin heard a clattering somewhere, the sound of someone typing at a computer keyboard. He read the black painted numbers on the glass of the office doors: 311, 309, 307 . . . So the professor's office was at the other end of the hall. Kevin almost ran to it.

The nameplate said, *Cornelia Lopez, Professor of Linguistics*. Kevin tried to look through the glass, but it was hard to see through. So he just sniffled what he hoped was his final sniffle and knocked on the door.

After a moment a woman impatiently said, "Come in," and so Kevin went in, carefully opening the door so that he did not, with any squeak of a hinge, disturb the quiet of the hall.

Once he was in, and the door shut behind him, he just stood silently, waiting for the professor to look his way. She was working at her desk, writing this and that. When she glanced up she was startled. "Who are you?" she asked. For a moment, Kevin smiled uncomfortably— and then he sniffled! Then he sneezed. Into his hand. He finally managed to tell her his name. His hand was wet with spray.

Professor Lopez could not imagine what business a boy could have with her. "What is it?" she asked. "Who sent you?"

Kevin suddenly realized he didn't know the cabbie's name, so he pretended that no one had sent him. He just said, "I need your help."

Professor Lopez squinted at Kevin, as if she were trying to wish him away. When he remained standing in front of her door, the professor sighed. "Do you know how busy I am?" she snapped.

Kevin shook his head.

"I am monstrously busy," she said. "I am terribly behind. I have papers to read. Students to fail. Research to nurture. You are interrupting me, little boy."

Kevin wiped his wet hand discreetly on the back of his right pants leg. "I just need your help," he said.

"My help."

Kevin nodded.

"Do you know what I do here?"

Kevin shrugged. "Linguistics."

"Which is — ?"

"I don't know. Language."

"Hmmm." The professor put down her pencil. She made a bothered face. And then, waving her hand once, she motioned for Kevin to come to her desk. Kevin did. Once there, he put out the letter for Professor Lopez to read. The professor took it.

"It's this letter," he said. "I need it analyzed."

The professor raised an eyebrow. "Analyzed."

"Yes. It doesn't make sense. It's messy."

"It doesn't make sense."

Kevin disliked the way she was echoing him. "Yeah, it doesn't make sense."

"Oh, indeed." She tossed the letter, without even reading it, onto her desk, and got a sheet of paper from a drawer. "Read this, if you want nonsense."

Kevin took the paper and read it. It *was* nonsense. He could barely read it. In fact, he read only about six or seven words before the nonsense stopped him dead. But then he felt the professor glaring at him, and so he read it all, to the very last word. So that you can properly feel sorry for Kevin, I ask you now to read it all as did he, right to the very last word of Professor Lopez's paragraph of nonsense, which was this:

> small to the off But buried again raining because and or the trunk head all using spiders even had video a nose which that feeling lost the he thrash leaf

The professor said, "I had an accident one day. All the words fell out of my books. I came into my office one morning and there they were, all the words, covering the shelves and floors like a black, slippery ash. It took me six months to get all the words back where they belonged. For six months I'd find words in my clothes, in my hair, on my food. I tried to keep them all in the office, but because I was working with so many, some inevitably stuck to me, and I'd carry them wherever I went. After I was done, after I *thought* I was done, I found those words"—she pointed to the paper in Kevin's hand—"in various places, at various times. I'm sure that many others are still lost somewhere. I have never felt altogether comfortable with my books since that accident.

"But in any event, *that's* nonsense, little boy. I had an office full of it once."

The professor took the paper back from Kevin. She looked at it for a moment or two. Oddly enough she then became distant, almost wistful, forgetful of Kevin standing there. "Poor orphans . . ." she said.

Kevin sneezed. The professor scowled, remembering he was there. She hastily forgot her wistfulness, shoved the paper of orphaned words back into her desk, and snatched up Kevin's letter from where it lay. She read it. "Hmmm. Yes, it is messy, as you say. But structurally, and apart from one word, it's quite unremarkable."

It was as if she had never spoken of the accident with her books. Back to the unpleasant business, it seemed. Well, that was fine with Kevin. He'd had no response to her bizarre story anyhow. No response was really possible to anything so bizarre.

He wondered which word she found

remarkable. Maybe it was *whale*. Maybe, as the cabbie had suggested, *whale* was an English-looking foreign word.

Kevin said, "One word? You mean the one that looks like *whale*?"

"*Whale*? No, that's just *whale*. I meant this middle word."

Ah! thought Kevin. *Kiss or kill.*

"I mean," said the professor, "I have never heard of the verb *to kirr*."

Kirr?!

"There aren't any words in English," she went on, "that end in double *r*. Not that I recall. Perhaps it is a foreign word, but even then, it is unfamiliar to me. It must have something to do with whales. Kirr, kirr, kirr," she said, giving the curious word a taste. "How does one kirr a whale? What does it involve? Is kirring a good thing, or bad? Can it be done without tools? Must the whale still be alive?"

Angrily Kevin grabbed the letter back from the professor. "It doesn't say *kirr*!"

"Pardon me, little boy," she said icily, "but I am the one doing the analysis here."

"But there's no such word as *kirr*!"

"Perhaps now there is! Every word has to have a birth, you know. Words come and go like people. Perhaps this *kirr* is newborn. Let me have that letter. I need to study it. I need it as evidence. The first documented usage of *kirr* . . ."

"It's not *kirr*! It's *kiss*!"

The professor laughed. "*Kiss*? Why in the world would you kiss a whale? Who kisses whales? It's not done."

In a huff, Kevin turned and noisily left the professor's office, clattering the old doorknob, squealing the hinges, slamming the door. The professor, once Kevin was gone, harumphed and went back to her work.

Outside, the cabbie was gabbing with three students, all of them young women. He was talking about his own days not so long ago at this very university, how everything was different now, but still the same. When Kevin, dark cloud on his face, came up, the cabbie said, "Well, ladies, gotta go. My fare is back," and the students said "Hi" to Kevin and "See ya later" to the cabbie, and drifted onward to class.

"So, Kevin. Any luck?"

"No."

"She couldn't help?"

"She wouldn't. She was dumb."

"Oh."

Kevin sat down on the curb and frowned. The cabbie, still standing, leaned with one arm on the top of the cab, and looked out into space, over the autumn campus.

"Well, what do you want to do now?"

Kevin didn't know. He really had no idea. He'd taken off for this town without any plan as such. He had thought that once he was in town, his next step would be clear.

Finally Kevin muttered, "*All* the words are wrong."

"What?"

"All the words in the letter. It's so sloppy it could say anything. It doesn't say *kiss*, or *kill*, or *whale*, or *must*, or *you*. It can't. That'd be stupid. It just says something else. And it doesn't matter anyway. It's just a joke. It's just a stupid joke." Kevin stood up. "It doesn't say *whale* or anything else. I want to go home."

Before the cabbie could reply, the three students he had been talking with came running up the sidewalk. When they saw that the cabbie and Kevin were still there, they stopped and one of them asked, "Did you hear?"

"Hear what?"

"On the beach! A whale's washed up on the beach."

"Yeah," said the second student. "It must have happened early this morning."

The third student said, "And it's still alive!"

"Come on!" all three of them cried.

The students ran to the beach. Kevin and the cabbie, for several moments, simply stared at each other.

The two-lane road went alongside the dunes, which sloped down to the water for several hundred feet. The crowd, come to see the whale, was already huge, and traffic choked the humble road. The cab in which Kevin and the cabbie sat was trapped like a brick in a wall. Overhead, two helicopters were circling — one from the Coast Guard and another that was unmarked.

Even in the cab, some distance up the road, they could hear the hum of the people down on the beach. And while the cabbie muttered, "Amazing, amazing," Kevin felt a shiver. Maybe it was a shiver left over from his sickness. But he did feel odd, as if a ghost had touched him. The letter didn't seem so stupid anymore.

The cab did not even inch forward. It only vibrated in place, its engine throbbing. Finally the cabbie said to Kevin, "Maybe you should just walk the rest of the way."

All of a sudden Kevin didn't want to set out anywhere on his own. He didn't want to be separated from the cabbie, who was at the moment his only friend. So Kevin shook his head no.

"But you should," said the cabbie. "It's all too weird, getting that letter, and then this. Too coincidental. You have to go down there."

"Alone?"

The cabbie shrugged. "Well, I can't very well just leave my cab here. Besides, you'll be okay."

"I'm only ten."

"That didn't stop you from sneaking away to a coastal town."

The cabbie wasn't scolding Kevin, not at all. He was, in fact, smiling kindly. Full of encouragement. Kevin realized that the cabbie was right.

Kevin made sure he had the letter in his pocket and then got out of the cab. Thinking for some reason that he might not see the cabbie again, he took his lunch bag and backpack, and tried to pay his fare. The cabbie laughed.

"Do you think you owe me a fare?"

"Well, yes . . ."

"You don't have nearly enough money."

"I don't?"

"Of course not."

"But I showed you what I had . . . Why did you pick me up?"

"Because you seemed so set upon something. I could tell you weren't running away. I've picked up runaways before. But you were on your own and headed somewhere. I was intrigued."

"But you're not supposed to give free rides."

"Well, yes, but who cares? Maybe I'll get reprimanded for it, maybe not. Maybe I'll pay the fare myself. But never mind about that. Just go, before the whale dies."

Kevin didn't know what to say. He just nodded, waved good-bye to the cabbie, and set out for the beach.

I've run out of paper. Those last fifty words or so are squeezed onto the final sheet. I squeezed them on because I wanted to finish the scene.

I need more paper. Mother has a lot, but it's hers, and she'd notice immediately if any sheets were missing.

It's also very dark in the broken room. The storm is seven days away. The clouds are warty looking, blackening, agitated. The sunlight's all but gone. And since none of the outlets in the room are intact, I can't take a lamp in there. I'd use a candle but I can't find any, and I certainly can't ask Mother where one is, because then she'd ask me what I needed it for.

Same problem with flashlights.

Except for the ones in Mother's chest.

But they need batteries.

So I need paper *and* batteries.

Fortunately, at dinner today, Mother let slip that tomorrow she's making a trip into Soso. She also needs some things to finish up her work. Besides that, we need to make a supply run before the storm hits. Once the storm's here, we'll be trapped in the house for a week and a half, and we can't afford to come up short on our spaghetti and salad.

◼ four

I dressed Zack for the trip. He's really so small. He's not smaller than any other baby his age, so far as I know; he's just so much smaller than me. When it was time to put on his shoes I put him in my lap, as if I were a chair, and I reached around him to tie his laces. Once the laces were tied I kept my arms where they were. Zack fit perfectly into my hug.

Myself I dressed with indifference, since there's no point in looking good for strangers. I didn't even comb my hair.

Mother wore a hat. Otherwise you'd not have known she was leaving the house to go to town.

The pickup coughed a lot, having sat unused in the living room for nearly three and a half weeks. When Mother threw it into gear we almost hit a wall. The ride along the driveway, through the broken rooms, was rough, not least because Mother floored the accelerator. We were doing sixty when we emerged from the house.

Then Mother aimed for Soso and accelerated to eighty-five. Either she was in a hurry or just didn't care. There's not much traffic in this desert, anyhow. And certainly no traffic cops. And tumbleweeds don't complain when you run them over.

The trip into Soso, at eighty-five miles an hour, took about twenty minutes. On the way there it was drizzling. The storm's drizzle. The edge of the rain. We went to one of those giant stores that sell everything: food, clothes, furniture, auto parts, ingredients for Ultimate Raincoats . . .

By the way, it's not like anyone in Soso knows who we are. When we come into town nobody whispers, "Oh, it's them, they're back, the squatters from the old desert house." No one knows we're in the house. Few, I bet, know the house is there. And there are enough people in town that being unknown is not remarkable.

Mother, Zack, and I are like any other mother and children come in from the neighborhoods to shop in Soso's stores.

I was worried about the paper and batteries. I didn't want Mother to know why I needed them, but I also didn't want to lie. I decided that I had to sneak the paper and batteries into the shopping cart. I hoped that Mother wouldn't notice. The grocery bill is pretty much the same every time, but perhaps, given the odd things (whatever they were) that Mother was buying for her work, the bill would be unusual anyhow and my contributions would go unnoticed.

So I had to do some sneaking. And I was worrying about it so much that when we came out at the end of an aisle and turned to go into the next, I didn't at first even recognize the girl at the other end of the store. Then her image caught up with me.

It was Michelle. There in the store.

Michelle was in the store!

I didn't leap from my mother to see if the girl was really Michelle. I didn't fly to the other end of the store. I was too keyed up for stealth, calm, and discretion. I guess I was also in shock.

Because it was *impossible*. We were a thousand miles from our old home. In a town beside a desert. In one of the town's hundred stores. And yet who should I come upon but my best friend Michelle?

It was impossible.

But after only a moment I slipped from my mother, and once out of her sight I *did* run, and fast, toward the other end of the store. I sideswiped a woman. She snapped at me, the witch. A clerk told me to slow down. I didn't.

I came up to where the girl had been, but she was gone. I looked down the nearest aisle. I saw her. Frantic, I almost cried out to her. I almost cried out *Michelle*! But then she turned and turned out to be no one I had ever known.

Just some stranger girl.

I was crushed. Only when I realized Michelle was still a thousand miles away did I realize how much I wished she weren't. I was angry at the stranger girl for resembling Michelle. I felt stupid for having made a mistake, for having nearly embarrassed myself. I'd been tricked by my own wishes. I'd wanted to see Michelle, and see her I did, even though she wasn't really there.

Sick in my heart, I returned to my mother. She asked where I'd been. "Nowhere," I said. She didn't ask anything more, and we finished our shopping as if nothing had happened. For my mother, of course, nothing had.

I then escaped being heartsick by concentrating again on stealth. I still needed my paper and batteries, after all. And indeed I got them into the cart, and Mother didn't notice. Back at home I got them out of the bag, and Mother didn't notice.

And now it's night. I still miss Michelle. I still hurt from this afternoon. Yet Michelle and the hurt don't seem to coincide as much anymore. Her image slips in and out, but the longing never weakens; and whenever her image is gone I discover, where she was standing, not the stranger girl but everything and everyone I want returned to me.

▬▬

After some fumbling about, I finally jammed one of Mother's flashlights, enlivened by batteries, into a crack in a wall and used it as if it were an overhead lamp. I really needed it, too. The sky is glutted with clouds, and day and night blur together.

I sat myself away from the open end of the broken room. The rain, which is stronger now, was whirling around the shredded wall and through some gaps in the ceiling. I stayed dry where I worked, although I did get a chill.

I worked very hard. Little time is left. What's more, this afternoon, as Mother had determined (using the almanac and her own observations), a squall was coming, a sort of sneeze before the greater blowout of the central storm. Several squalls, in fact, starting at 4:26 P.M. I knew this because Mother had noted the details on the kitchen calendar. The squalls would reach through the room even to where I was, in my dry corner, so I had to hurry.

I hurried. And today I reached the end of Father's story.

Kevin had set out for the beach, and then—

> A policeman stopped him. There were lots of policemen around. Their cars, with red and blue lights flashing, were scattered everywhere. Unauthorized people had not yet been barred from the beach, but the police were nevertheless trying to control the crowd. For example, by stopping boys who were running past.
>
> "Hey, kid, you can't go down there."
>
> "I just want to see—"
>
> "You can see well enough from here."
>
> "But my dad's down there—"
>
> "Then wait for him up here."
>
> So the lie about his dad didn't work. Fine. Kevin just bolted from the policeman (who

called out uselessly) and disappeared into the forest of adults.

Television cameramen with video cameras on their shoulders and wires trailing in the sand were stumbling over the dunes. Some newscasters already had their teams set up against a backdrop of the stranded whale, and were broadcasting to their viewers. All around the whale were clumps of people, apparently arguing. Here and there were people touching the whale. Some were poking it, to see if it would react. Others were trying to cut off a piece as a souvenir. The teeth, especially, were sought after as valuable, and as soon as a policeman snatched one vandal from the whale's mouth, another slithered up, hammer and saw in hand.

Some people, apparently drunk, were walking on top of the whale and throwing cans down onto the beach.

"It's a sperm whale," said someone behind Kevin.

Kevin turned, and there was a dirty, shabbily clothed man standing less than a foot away.

"Look how big it is," said the man.

Kevin stepped away from the man, but did look at the whale as the man had directed. Of course Kevin saw its size. The whale rose like a black hillock from the sand. But what caught

Kevin was not so much the whale's size, as its *life*. Although it was firmly held to the ground by its own tremendous weight, the whale had not stopped moving altogether. Its eyes moved and watched. Through the blowhole, every so often, a blast of air came. And with its giant flukes the whale occasionally slapped the beach, sending a shudder through the legs of everyone nearby.

"It won't survive," said the man.

Kevin stared at him.

"It won't survive," he repeated. "Do you see those people over there? Volunteers. They brought towels to soak in the sea and place on the whale to cool it. Didn't do much good. Really couldn't. They talked about using a helicopter to lift the whale back into the water. No go. They tried ropes to drag it back in, but the ropes just cut into its skin. What they can't accept is that the whale was as good as dead as soon as it hit the beach."

Kevin didn't like the man and started to move away from him. But then the man said, "Wait a minute, Kevin. You did get my letter, didn't you?"

The sight of the whale had unsettled Kevin enough. Now he had to learn that the person who had sent the letter was a shabby, greasy, stained and torn, craggy, wrinkled, stupidly grinning old and wobbling *bum*.

Kevin forgot his resentment. He did not want to confront anyone anymore. He did not want to demand an explanation. The man just didn't seem worth the anger, for he was as much a mess as the letter he had sent.

"I knew the whale was going to do that," said the man. "Do you want to know how I knew?"

Kevin slowly nodded.

"I'm omniscient. You know what that means?"

Kevin slowly shook his head.

"It means I know everything. I am aware of everything. I am an omniscient bum. I mean, I'm not omniscient because I'm a bum. Being a bum does nothing for your brain. I ought to know." He grinned stupidly. "No, I'm omniscient because I am. Like, I've got brown eyes because I do. I was born that way."

The man watched Kevin for a moment. Kevin wasn't visibly reacting; he seemed in a daze. The man burped, then went on.

"No, really, I'm omniscient. I'm not omnipotent, mind you. I'm omniscient. I just know everything. I can't *do* everything. I can't change spiders into ice cream cones, or stuff like that. Though I wish I could. Ah, to go to Saturn in the summer! I'd love to see the rings up close. If I was omnipotent I could go, just as I please, but I am only powerless, as powerless as you."

Kevin glared at the man. "What do you mean?"

"Why, um . . . Powerless, I mean. Like, there's nothing you can do for that whale. To save it, I mean. Sometimes whales just strand themselves, you know. There's simply no saving them. The whale's own weight is destroying it even now.

"I mean, you see those people arguing over there? They're not arguing about how to save the whale. They're scientists who want to get samples. Scientists don't know a lot about sperm whales, and all this is quite an opportunity. For research, you know. But you can't blame them for being scientists. I mean, they just want to find out how the whale works.

"Some of those other people are public officials, trying to figure out how to get rid of the whale once it is dead. They're afraid it will become a public health hazard.

"But in any event, that whale cannot be saved."

Kevin said, "So I should go kill it?"

I said I reached the end of Father's story. I did not say I reached the finish. That is where it ends. The last eight words on the final sheet. There isn't any more. It's crazy. My father just stopped. In the middle of the sheet. There's nothing on the back, even. He just stopped.

Why would he do that?

And why would Mother keep an unfinished story?

For that matter, why would she keep anything of Father's? She considers him dead and properly gone. I know he's just run away again, maybe for good, but he isn't dead. I know he isn't. But if Mother has buried him before his death, why should she care for any reminder of him? You'd think she'd have burned the story or something.

But of course, the chest itself is unusual. My mother has never seemed nostalgic. Although neatly arranged, the things in her chest have no order, no place with each other, except as debris, apparently, of her life. Memories to put in your hand.

And, at least for me, most of those memories are obscure. Things like the pencil case I can understand. It's mine, she got it for me, it's from when I was only nine, a little girl. But the scarecrow doll? That was never mine. Was it hers? And the string of bells? The earring with the orange feather? The small bundle of toothpicks? (There's a bundle of toothpicks in there!)

And why would she keep a bunch of ancient flashlights?

But keeping the story especially bewilders me. Why keep around an unfinished story?

Unless Mother hasn't quite buried my father.

■■

The squalls prevented me from thoroughly searching the chest for the rest of Father's story.

At dinner Mother grumbled about her Raincoat. She said it was shoddy and would never work. Since I was worrying about the story I wasn't really listening. Of course Mother wasn't really talking to me. She muttered something about starting over and left her plate behind, untouched.

The squalls ended soon after dinner. I put Zack in his crib and went back to the broken room.

I didn't expect to find the rest of Father's story, but I had to try. I had to know. I got reckless in my search. I paid no attention to Mother's neatness. After all this time I rifled through the chest as if no one else would ever go through it again.

I found a lot more of Mother's life in there, but I did not find the rest of Father's story. I guess I've already found all that I am going to find.

Now what do I do?

■ ■

I'm bored again. No more story, no more writing, my time's so empty now, and by and large I'm little more than bored, bored, bored. So today, to *do* something, I went out to Mother's tent. I didn't go to *see* her. I went to *spy* on her. I went late this morning, rather suddenly in fact. I was just wilting on the couch when I heard a thud outside. I knew it wasn't the storm, since a storm, even this one, never thuds. Mother must have dropped something large, and not for the first time I wondered what she was up to. This time I decided to find out.

Mother has a path through the house, through the broken rooms, out into the yard and from there to her tent. We created this path the day after we created the driveway. For two days we cleared away walls and beams and shattered floors as though they were jungle vines and bushes. In a way it had been fun.

I've barely ever used the path myself.

At the yard I slowed down. It was pouring. I crossed the yard cautiously, spy that I was. I drew myself along the tent's canvas side, listening for Mother. She was inside the tent. She was moving things around. I crouched down, lifted the canvas slightly, and lowered my head to look through. I was so awkwardly positioned I fell over. With an ache in my shoulder I then lay on my stomach, down in the mud, and spied.

If Mother had dropped something, she had already picked it up, or so it seemed. I disregarded that anonymous thud and tried to find Mother's Ultimate Raincoat. I looked and I looked, but the only thing I saw that might have been the coat was a tall thing in the middle of the tent. That thing was covered with a sheet, however, so I really couldn't tell what it was.

I gave up looking and watched Mother instead.

She was fussing over her equipment. She really does have a lot of it, all webbed with wires and pocked with lights. Lots of tools, too, and lots of materials and scrap. I've never liked that kind of stuff myself. I don't recall Father much liking it either. Machines were always Mother's business. She understood them. She was always rebuilding our appliances, making them do things they hadn't been built to do.

She often lost patience with Father, who obstinately refused to understand her work. They often bickered over machinery, of all things. They never got angry exactly, but I don't know why they kept it up. Maybe they were teasing each other. Or maybe they were, more than anything else, reminding each other of their differences. So long as Mother and Father kept in mind that they were different, separate people, their frequent separations would be that much easier to bear.

That's what I was thinking as I lay there in the mud and rain, spying on my mother the busy lunatic. Mother is not, of course, bearing the current separation very well.

I wondered what she was up to. She was closing panels, latching covers, coiling up the power cords. Then it dawned on me: She was *packing*, and she only does that when a new Raincoat is ready. She was getting all her stuff out of the storm's way.

So soon my mother, like me, will have nothing to do, and we can be bored together.

■ five

Zack is asleep.

The storm, its core, is two days away. The core is twenty miles across. Only part of it will touch us, but that part will be enough.

Mother has finished her Raincoat. Or so I presume. She's moved all her equipment back into the house, and she's not going out to her tent anymore. She's not doing anything anymore. She just wanders around the house, room to room, picking up things, putting them down, trailing her fingers along the walls. Whenever I try to talk to her she just stares at me in surprise, as if one of the chairs has spoken up. At dinner she doesn't speak, she doesn't let a word slip out. I give her cold spaghetti and she eats it.

Father's unfinished story lies under my bed.

I'm sitting on the broken porch, watching the wind tug at the ruined juniper trees. The rain carries deep into the porch and ends as a mist on my face and arms. I look out to the distant mesas. I want to get up, walk straight toward them, get lost in the desert under the storm.

Zack is still asleep. I wish I was.

■■

This morning Mother was muttering numbers to herself. I don't know what they meant, exactly. Something to do with the storm, which will be here tomorrow. Mother looked to the ceiling and muttered number after number.

I gave Zack his breakfast. Oatmeal. I remember when I was little I would sit alone every morning at my own little table, a table low enough for me to reach its top while sitting on the floor, and at my table in front of the television I would eat three or four bowls of oatmeal. Mother made them for me. She must have. Father was gone at the time.

I wiped Zack's face when he was done eating. Then I passed the backs of my fingers once across his cheek. His cheek was cool and smooth. Cool and smooth, I thought, like porcelain.

Poor Zack. I wondered if he would ever know

Father. Zack had only one parent, his mother, and the closest she had come to him in so many months had been through her abandoned scarecrow doll. I wanted to give Zack the doll then, never mind the consequences. I wanted to give him everything in Mother's chest, every piece of Mother he could have. The doll, the flashlights, the string of bells . . .

Mother's muttering of numbers began to irritate me. I wanted her just to *speak,* and speak to me. To get out of her storm-set mind. I wanted her to—

Just then my mind was pricked by a clever and subversive thought. I grinned at it. The bells. I would give Zack the string of bells, tie them to his sleeves and his shoes, so that whenever he moved there would be a bellish noise.

And Mother would hear. She would see the bells, recognize them as hers. From her chest. She would know then that I had gone into her chest. I knew that all my talking to her would never accomplish a thing; but the noise of the bells and her anger at their presence would surely make Mother speak to me.

■■

Of course I first had to get to the chest. I didn't want Mother to see me go or return, since I wanted

72

the bells to be a shock, wholly unexpected. Mother *had* to go on with her distant muttering, without a thought for me at all.

But when could I go?

Then I realized that Mother would be out in her tent today, putting on her Raincoat, because the core of the storm was due to arrive. I could go to the broken room while she was away.

Mother left early this morning. For the trip to the tent she wore a simple, normal raincoat, because that was all she needed, the storm's core being, as of then, some time away. As Mother left she said only one thing: "No more defeats." She said this boldly, I thought. I waited five minutes until I was sure she had left the house. I put Zack in his playpen and set out for the chest.

I got the bells. The wind and rain were stirring the room, but the chest stayed heavily where it was, right where it had sat through eleven passings of the storm.

On my way back through the broken rooms I saw Mother beside her tent, still in her simple, normal raincoat. I peered at her through two hanging boards. She had collapsed her tent, which now lay, poles and canvas, in the mud. I didn't see anything else. I knew all the equipment was gone—but I had expected to see the Ultimate Raincoat, perhaps that tall thing that had been under the sheet.

Yet nothing was there.

I waited for the coat to rise out of the ground, or fall from the sky, or something. It didn't. I squinted at the patch of desert that had been inside the tent, but there was nothing there at all.

Mother stared at the nothingness, nodded twice, then headed quickly to the house. For a moment, still bewildered, I forgot that I was not with Zack. I was, that is, where I shouldn't have been—and Mother was returning to the inner rooms.

I ran. Boy, did I ever.

■■

I ran too fast. I tripped on a hole in the floor and fell down, hurting my knee and scraping the palms of my hands. That slowed me down, enough to allow Mother to get back before me.

She was sitting on the couch, facing Zack in his playpen. When I stumbled in, wet and somewhat bleeding, Mother heard and turned to look, but apart from a brief, quizzical squint, she didn't really react. I walked past her and Zack and sat in a chair. Then, for several minutes, the only sounds were Zack's and the storm's.

The core was over us. The house shuddered.

"I finished my raincoat," said Mother, calmly.

She meant her Ultimate Raincoat. I nodded.

"It's outside. Or maybe I should say it's not. But it is."

I thought, *If it is, then where is it?*

Mother said, "It really is there. Although it's not. But I bet you think that I don't have my raincoat at all. Isn't that what you think?"

I shrugged. "I dunno—"

"But I do have one! One that the storm can't harm, can't even *touch*. It's a raincoat that *isn't there*."

I stared at her.

"And that's why I'm *here* inside the house," she said, "while my raincoat is outside in the storm. Only a person who *isn't there* can wear a raincoat that *isn't there*.

"And look how dry I am!" she cried.

I had no answer to that. Mother meant it. She'd finally succeeded. She beamed at me in her success. I smiled back weakly, and after a while I took Zack away and left her alone.

But Mother glowed happily for hours, there on the couch, as she wore her most ultimate raincoat and the storm devoured the world outside.

■ ■

My plan for the bells just fell apart. It seemed so *angry* all of a sudden, and therefore inappropriate. Mother had finally gone over the edge, or so at the time it seemed to me. No point in being angry at someone in her condition.

The days went on, each as bad as the one before. We heard the broken rooms breaking more. The rain, the hail, pounded the roof. The wind bent the house this way and that. Water dripped from every crack, and puddles slickened the floors. We had to sleep wherever it was dry, and eventually we ended up in the same room, Zack's room, which was the driest.

Mother still wandered about, speaking little to me. I was not, however, as infuriated as I had been. *Let her wander,* I thought. Whatever the madwoman wants.

I even gave her dinners that weren't at all cold, although the storm sometimes did make them a little wet.

Sleeping in the same room with Zack and Mother was hard. I mean, it was hard enough with the storm rioting all around us regardless of the hour. On top of that there was my brother, waking up every hour because of the storm, and my mother lying all of five feet away from me. If I didn't need to be dry while sleeping . . .

But then last night I awoke, only halfway to dawn, to find Mother missing from her makeshift bed. I looked up and saw her at Zack's crib. She was holding him and rocking him gently, and through the riotous grumble of the storm I heard my mother singing a tiny lullaby.

And tonight I am again awake too early, and five feet from me I hear my mother sobbing, over what I don't know.

■■

On the fairest summer days, and even those less fair, and sometimes during the fall (after school), my father would more or less skip work and take me to the airport. I say more or less because although he was out on a legitimate errand for his store (he was picking up books from the warehouse), he didn't return straightaway but came home and got me and strayed, for half an hour or so, to watch the planes come and go.

The airport was a small one, no jumbo jets, no jets at all, no airplanes, in fact, with more than four seats. Most of the planes were parked on the grass. The hangars were old and made of sheet metal. Father would park the van full of books on the shoulder of the road, and we would get out and walk into the nearby field, and then we'd sit down together and wait for the shadows of wings to flash over us.

I think my father liked his job. He certainly bought a lot of books. I read most of those that I could. But there he was, goofing off on company time and stealing me, without Mother's knowledge, for an afternoon. Mother never found out. Father and I kept our secret.

Now when I remember the airport, I realize that I have no such memories of Mother and me. She never stole me for an afternoon; she's only kidnapped me for a year. But I realize also that I want such memories.

The field, the wings, but this time with my mother.

Some distant afternoon.

■ ■

I had hidden the bells in my room. It had been too unsafe, during the storm, to go back to the chest. Today, however, only the tail of the storm was dragging over us: the rain and wind dozing off, the clouds breaking from each other, the sunlight reaching through. It was safe enough to return the bells.

Except that Mother was there.

I had thought she was holed up in her room. She *had* been. I hadn't seen her leave. I thought I could sneak out to the broken room and get back without any problems.

But there was Mother, *right beside her chest*.

When I saw her my heart just about jumped out of my body. I nearly tripped. I stumbled backwards. I shot back into the hall and tried to catch my breath. I prayed that Mother hadn't seen or heard me.

I don't think she had.

I peered through the torn wall. The chest wasn't open or anything. Mother sat, her back to me, her knees pulled up to her chin. She was very still, as still as the chest, as still as the broken room.

I moved back from the wall and climbed carefully, quietly, over the debris to a different place. I was farther away but I could still see her.

Mother didn't move. A couple of times she rubbed her nose. She let her legs out once and soon pulled them back. But she stayed where she was. She never touched the chest. She never stopped looking at it, though.

I waited for her to open it.

I imagined her picking out Father's story, which was right on top of everything else. I imagined her reading it. She must be better with Father's handwriting than I am. But would she *want* to read the story? I'm sure she's read it before, but would she read it now? It's not only unfinished—it's kind of sad, the way it is. It stops unhappily. It doesn't make any sort of decision, and I know that bothers *me*.

But in any event, she didn't read it. She didn't do much of anything. After a while, although I had wanted to learn what she was doing there, I knew I had to leave. I was surely risking some sort of confrontation by staying, and I was in no mood for any sort of confrontation. So I left.

I'll just have to return the bells tomorrow.

■■

Two days in a *row* Mother scares me to death!

Yes, I know, I should have returned the bells this morning, right away, as soon as I was able. But I wasn't feeling brave. I just couldn't forget that scare I got yesterday. I simply needed the time to work up some courage.

But then what does Mother do? While I'm sitting at the kitchen table, making courage, she comes in *with the bells*.

She sat across from me and put the bells down on the table. I should have realized she might have found them. Now that the storm is finishing up, Mother has been assessing the damage to the inner rooms. I guess that in my room she assessed a little too closely and found the bells.

She did not, however, find my copy of Father's story.

I slowly looked up. My heart was frantic. But Mother wasn't mad. She calmly asked me, "Why do you have these?"

I didn't tell her about my plan! I just said, "I dunno. They're pretty. I like them."

"Why were you in my chest?"

All she meant, really, was, *I don't know how you found my chest, Evelyn, but you know that you shouldn't have gone into it and taken out what wasn't yours.* I, however, took her question to mean, *What were you doing with my chest, Evelyn, all those days in the broken room?*

I said, "I was reconstructing Father's story."

That startled her. "What story?" she muttered.

"The one about the whale."

Mother was dumbfounded. She sagged in her chair.

I couldn't quite understand her reaction. I had probably touched something much too private. She said, "You were doing *what* to it?" "Reconstructing it," I said. "What do you mean?" she asked. I told her Father's handwriting was awful. She laughed slightly at that.

"It doesn't have an ending," I said.

"What?"

"There's no ending."

She nodded. "I know."

I wasn't sure I should press her, but after all my work, I *needed* to know. "Do *you* know the ending?" I asked.

"No," she said.

I waited for her to continue, but she didn't.

"So there isn't an ending at all?"

"No, there isn't." And she asked sourly, "Does it matter?"

I shrugged. It *did* matter, but apparently only to me.

For a while we sat, saying nothing, until Mother asked, "Why did you—*reconstruct* that story?"

"I just wanted to. I dunno."

"You should have left it alone."

"Sorry."

"Don't apologize."

"Sorry . . ."

"Should've left it alone," she said.

"I guess so."

"You *guess* so? You should have."

"All right, I should have."

"It's just trash—"

"Then why did you keep it?"

That was the wrong thing to ask. Mother glared at me. Then she said, "Why do you think?" She didn't actually want an answer to that. She just wanted me to shut up. I did. I shut up—especially because she started to sob. All of a sudden she sank into herself. I watched her sink. I didn't know what to do. All I did, at last, was lamely say, "Don't worry about it, Mom."

How that could have been comforting, I don't know. But soon her sobbing did let up. She wiped her eyes. Then she looked at me and said, "I'm so sorry, Evelyn. I'm so sorry I brought you here." And then, right away, she whispered, "Please don't ever run away from me."

Out of the blue she said that to me. I was still getting a grip on her surprising apology when she handed me her plea. I hesitated, and during my hesitation Mother took the bells, got up, and left the room. But I couldn't speak, nor cry out a thing to her, for my mind was too busy spitefully crying,

Just who's run away from who, anyhow? I hesitated too long—and Mother, too weakened to wait long for me, was gone.

■■

I have no right to be—there's no excuse—but I am often stupid nonetheless. Yet what was I supposed to do? My mother confuses me. Am I expected to understand her? I mean, she brings me here, tries to make a coat and can't, goes mad it seems, and then, coming into the kitchen, is as normal as can be. We get into a sort of fight. She turns to sobbing. She apologizes. Then she pleads.

And I'm supposed to keep up?

In these days since, I have not seen my mother once. I don't know where in the house she is, and I haven't looked. I don't know when she eats or sleeps, if she does at all. This void has, at least, given me time to catch up, to consider our encounter, to leave aside my stupidity. I think about what happened and, really, how much more obvious could it be? Mother has never stopped loving Father. She kept the story because it was *his*. And why wouldn't she sob? Being lonely, being wronged, she can cry without excuse. Being neglectful of me and Zack—

I don't say that now with spite. She knows of the neglect and regrets it. Clearly she does. But haven't I neglected her as well? Oh, part of me complains: I can't imagine *how*, for it seems to me that *she* has directed our exile here, and I have simply never protested . . . Doesn't it seem that way to you? Yet my being passive has made me less her daughter somehow and more just another of her possessions. She may have seldom talked to me, but I have seldom talked to her.

And so, plaintively she asks that *I* not leave *her*. As if I might. As if I was to her so distant that I might fall below the horizon one day and leave her utterly alone.

I can't read my mother's mind. I am only guessing about things. It's been so long, though, since I had anything good to base even a guess on. If not for the bells—if not for Father's story—

Endingless. Mother doesn't have the ending.

And so I guess I have to make one up myself.

"Kill it?" cried the bum. He was taken aback. "Whatever do you mean?"

"Your letter says I must kill a whale."

"Kill?"

"Yes. Doesn't it?"

"Why, no, of course not."

"Well, it's awfully hard to read."

"What is?"

"Your letter! What does it really say?"

The man was flabbergasted. After a moment he said, "Why, it says, You must kiss a whale."

"Just barely," said Kevin, frowning. "It's a mess."

The man shrugged. "Sorry. I guess I'm a messy person."

"But why must I kiss a whale?"

The man paused, and then leaning toward Kevin he said, "Because a kiss would comfort that poor whale."

"Comfort? The whale needs a kiss?"

"Of course. I mean, don't we all?"

And so, I guess, Kevin kisses the whale. It seems to me he would have, perhaps after first resenting the need to. Kevin goes past the scientists, policemen, vandals, and gawkers, and puts a hand against the whale, on its rough skin, maybe beside a scar left by a belligerent squid, and gives the whale a kiss. Some people laugh at Kevin. The policemen pull him away.

But Kevin is happy, and the whale is happy.

After that, what happens, I don't know.

■■

I found Mother in the broken room. With Zack in his papoose I'd gone looking for Mother and found her sitting, legs crossed, beside her chest. The chest was opened. Mother looked at me as I looked at her: with a stare. After a moment she returned to her rummaging.

I'd come to say something to her. To give her a reply. I walked up and stood a few steps in front of her. I wondered briefly if she had noticed the mess that I (and Zack) had made of her things. Perhaps she had. In any event she was making her own mess now: a pile of her things on the floor. I noticed the bells in the pile. Eventually I took Zack out of the papoose and set him down. He crawled to Mother and, after a moment of her halfhearted play with him, he crawled onward to the pile of things and played with them.

I said to Mother, "I won't run away."

She looked up. "What?"

"You asked me not to. I won't."

She looked down again. "Thank you," she said.

I moved closer and sat as she was sitting.

"We'll leave tomorrow," she told me, adding, "if you want."

Afraid to simply rejoice, I asked, "Where to?"

"Some place with normal weather," she said.

I said okay.

She paused. "A lot of junk here, isn't there?"

I shrugged. "Yeah, a lot."

Mother lifted one object up, then another, giving each a look, allowing each to work at her memory. She told me some fact or another about some of them. She showed me a one-page computer printout and asked me if I knew what it was. Of course I recognized it, having rifled through the chest. I could tell it was a listing of some computer program; but I can't read any computer language, and so I told my mother I had no idea what it was.

She smiled. Mother smiled. She said, "Bouncing line."

I almost said huh, but then I remembered.

When I was six years old, you see, Mother sat me on her lap in front of her computer and told me, with a grin, to press the letter E on the keyboard. E for Evelyn, she said; and I pressed the letter E; and on the video screen, inside a large square, a line an inch long appeared. This line began swirling within the square, spinning, bouncing off the sides, leaving a trail of other lines behind it. The line changed its color as it spun and bounced, and each line that was left behind kept the color of the moment before. Soon the bouncing line went away, and filling the square was a scatter of lines, an outcry of colors, a bright video rainbow for me, her little girl.

I'd forgotten all about that.

▪ epilogue

Last night Zack called me on the phone. It was rather late, nearly midnight, but after all, Mother always lets Zack stay up as late as he pleases. Zack is tireless. Mother's usually up herself until way past midnight, and she and Zack do make a busy, or at least lively, pair.

Zack asked me what I was doing. I told him I was studying for my final exams. He knows what those are. He asked me if there are final exams in first grade. He's going right now. I told him I didn't think so. He told me that Mother is trying to teach him about transistors again. He didn't say *transistors*. He said something garbled, but I knew what he meant, and I think he was just willfully mispronouncing the word. He does like wheels and gears and, curiously enough, flashlights too, but he doesn't care much for transistors.

He said he misses me and plans to write me a letter. He's just learning to write. He started last summer, started himself, after watching me scribble for hours on end. He wants to write me a letter because he misses me, but then he says writing is stupid and talking is better. So he puts off the letter writing and calls me on the phone.

Zack my brother, my father's son, thinks writing is stupid. What would Father say to that? I know Zack is mostly being just his ornery self, but even so, what would Father have thought? Of course I can't ask my father. He's still gone. But his absence has never stopped my wondering.

As Zack and I talked, I heard Mother in the background. She hollered hello to me. Zack and I talked some more. Eventually I had to tell him I had things to do, and he said so did he. So we said good-bye and together, reluctantly, we hung up.

■■

I remember when we went out to the desert. It was only days after Father had, yet again, disappeared—a short time after Zack was born. As usual Father was leaving things unfinished. That was his way. After three years of stability Mother had thought that our life was set at last, as though upon a river, straight and wide: here, going serenely and clearly there. I hadn't thought so much about it. Father was with us, that was that, maybe he'd leave, maybe he'd not. I had assumed those three years would not be all, that there would be more; but I hadn't thought about it much. I realize now I didn't want to. Mother, I suspect, didn't want to either, for somehow she knew that again we'd find ourselves to be passing not upon a river but through a puddle, one larger than the others but no less still and shallow.

So Father left, and we did too, and I instantly, and for months, blamed my mother. To me, Father's leaving was natural; ours was not. Mother *brought* me to the desert—I did not volunteer—so *she* got the blame. Father got my reminiscing, my reconstructing; Mother got my anger, bewilderment, and silence.

But in watching my mother's undoing of herself, down to the creation of things that were never there, I realized that blaming her was wrong, and blame, in any event, was itself irrelevant. My father should not be forgiven, I know, however much either of us might love him. He mistreated us. Nevertheless, after being so long inside his story (which I still have), I can in a way understand him. Can't quite forgive him, but can understand him, and can leave aside the blame.

Father was, all in all, a very sad person. He could imagine a kiss, he had even received a kiss (I'm thinking of our love for him, which, despite everything, persists); but he could never really hold that kiss. He had no faith in it. It always slipped away from him—and so always did he, far away from us.

I admit I am guessing again. Too little to go on, really. But I suppose that the guesses, having been made, should be left behind as is. Yes, more unfinished things! But a finish can't always be expected. Every day is the final day for one thing or another, finished or not. It's just that you must let the thing become unfinished on its own. Only then can you rightfully say, *I am leaving for good.*

Too often, I know, it's hard to judge when the time is right. Father was awful at judging the time to leave, the time to stay. Mother and I weren't always much better. But one day I sat with her and we agreed to leave the desert; and the next day, with Zack peacefully between us, we drove onward another thousand miles to where the weather is as normal as can be.

A few years later I graduated from high school. Now I'm in college. At one time I thought I'd never even make it to the eighth grade. But here I am, a genuine college student, studying off and on in my dormitory room. Zack will no doubt call me again tomorrow. He calls me every other day, more or less. He does miss me. I miss him, very much. But he knows where I am, and I know where he is. And we both know that in a few days, after my exams, I'll be coming home.

▪ about the author

David Skinner was born in 1963, grew up here and there in Michigan and Ohio, got a B.A. in History from the University of Michigan (although he started out in Honors Physics), worked as an assistant editor, never married, and is now pursuing a teaching certificate in hopes of someday teaching junior high school kids lots of history and a little mathematics, too. This is his first novel.